THIS IS A BORZOI BOOK PUBLISHED BY ALFRED A. KNOPF, INC.
Text copyright © 1992 by Daisaku Ikeda. Illustrations copyright © 1992 by Brian Wildsmith. English version copyright
© 1992 by Geraldine McCaughrean. First translated from the Japanese by Burton Watson. All rights reserved under
International and Pan-American Copyright Conventions. Published in the United States by Alfred A. Knopf, Inc., New York.
Distributed by Random House, Inc., New York. Originally published in Great Britain by Oxford University Press in 1992.
First American Edition 1993.   Manufactured in Hong Kong   10 9 8 7 6 5 4 3 2 1

Library of Congress Cataloging-in-Publication Data
Ikeda, Daisaku. Over the deep blue sea / by Daisaku Ikeda ; illustrated by Brian Wildsmith ; English version by Geraldine
McCaughrean.   p.   cm.   Summary: Prejudice linked to an event from the past threatens the friendship that Akiko and her
brother have made with a boy on their new island home.   ISBN 0-679-84184-9 (trade)   ISBN 0-679-94184-3 (lib. bdg.)
|1. Prejudices—Fiction. 2. Friendship—Fiction. 3. Islands—Fiction.| I. Wildsmith, Brian, ill.   II. McCaughrean, Geraldine.
III. Title. PZ7.I280v 1993 |E|—dc20 92-22557

Over the Deep Blue Sea

written by **DAISAKU IKEDA**   illustrated by **BRIAN WILDSMITH**

English version by Geraldine McCaughrean

ALFRED A. KNOPF   NEW YORK

Akiko and Hiroshi were awakened, on the morning of a new life, by the sound of the sea. Their parents' work had brought them to an island where green shade dappled golden sand and flowerheads brighter than butterflies wagged in the salty air.

"It will be perfect here," said Akiko, looking out at the ocean.

"If we can just make some friends," said her brother.

That was not so easy. The islanders' language was difficult to learn.
Some of the children were shy of this new girl and boy. Akiko and
Hiroshi were lonely at first.

Then along came Pablo—always smiling, always ready for a game.
Proud of his island, he showed Akiko and Hiroshi all its glorious secrets.

He showed them coves where pirates had once beached their ships, buried their treasure, and dined on coconuts and fruit. He showed them where freshwater streams trickled into the sea and made pale fissures of turquoise. He even taught them how to paddle a canoe!

One day he showed them a rusty red reef of twisted metal rearing up out of the sea—a wrecked ship groaning among the movement of the waves—while overhead the seabirds screamed.

"What ship is it?" whispered Akiko. "It gives me a bad feeling."

"I don't know," said Pablo. "But I'll ask my grandma. She knows all about the past."

Together they swam underneath the surface, and Pablo showed them shallows where the fish were even more colorful than the flowers on shore.

"I always thought the sea was just blue," said Hiroshi. "But look! There are purples and greens—and do you see those deep blue stripes?"

"Those are currents," said Pablo. "Be careful of those." But although Hiroshi nodded, he did not really understand that the sea is a country with rivers of its own: powerful rivers speeding through all the Seven Seas.

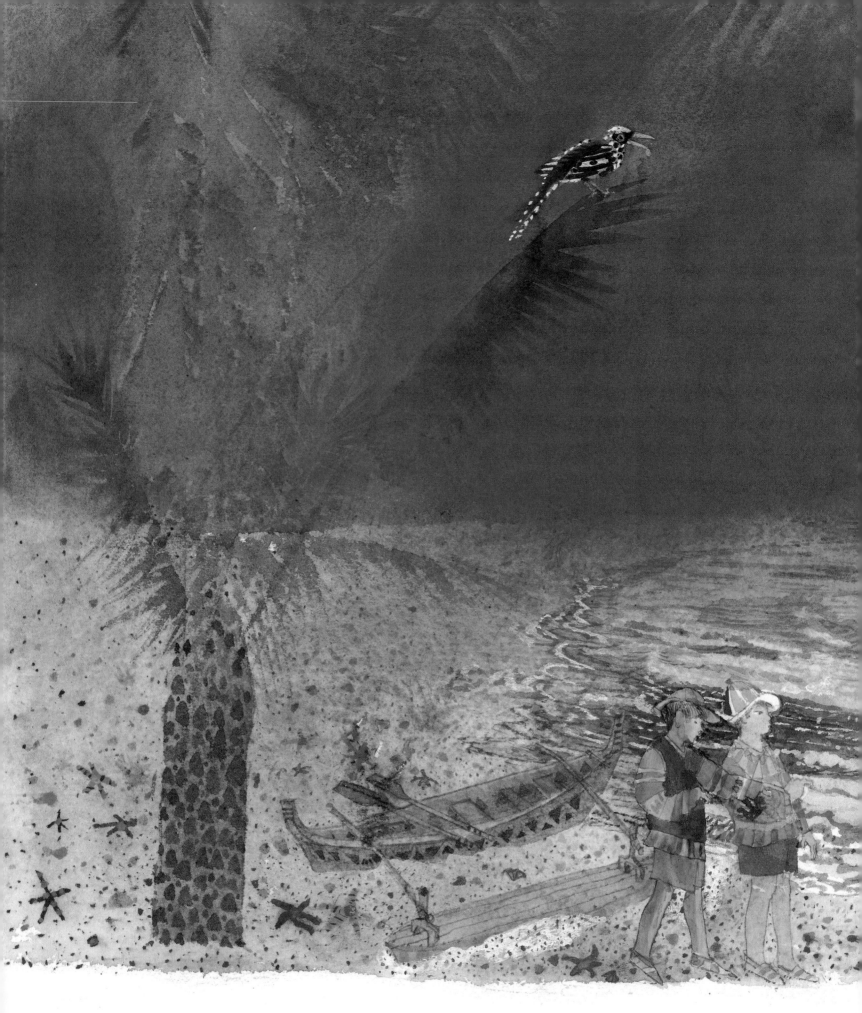

Then one dusk, Pablo showed them the most wonderful sight of all.
He took them to a beach where, by the last light of day, they saw a
hundred gentle creatures bumble clumsily ashore, their great curving
backs balanced on four stumpy legs. "Sea turtles," he said quietly.

"What strange animals! Why are they here?" breathed Akiko.

"Where do they come from?" asked Hiroshi.

"Far out at sea. But they always find their way here in time to lay their eggs. They've done it for a million years. Grandma told me," said Pablo.

Next day Pablo was not waiting on the beach as usual.

"It's too late to be watching the turtles," suggested Hiroshi.

They waited, but still Pablo did not come—not that day, nor the next. Finally they found him. To their amazement, he said, "I won't play with *you* anymore. I know what *you* are. I asked my grandma about that wreck in the bay. She told me how you came here in the war . . ."

"We *did*?"

"Your *kind*. People from your country. How you attacked our island. You're the enemy. It's one of your ships. I'm glad it sank."

"Who needs him?" said Hiroshi fiercely. "If we are Pablo's enemy, then he is ours."

"But I wanted him for a friend," sobbed Akiko. "Where are you going?"

"Out on the water."

"On your own?"

"Why not? Those clumsy old turtles have been doing it for a million years. I don't need Pablo. I don't need anyone!"

Akiko stood on the shore, watching her brother paddle his canoe angrily across the ocean's striped colors. The sky was striped too now, with black clouds and blowy rain. "Hiroshi, come back!"

Soon Hiroshi saw the sky turn a bleak black. He tried to turn back. But something was pulling the canoe, towing him out to sea. The waves crashed down upon him. His canoe began to groan and split. That great blue cord of ocean knotted itself around his legs, cold and sure.

"Here! Hiroshi! Swim to me! Over here!" It was Pablo.

Somehow Hiroshi pulled himself into Pablo's canoe. Together they battled against the boiling currents, against the wind, into walls of breaking water.

Though they paddled with all their might, they could not outpull the sea. Soon they were exhausted, blinded with spray, numb with cold, and the shore was nowhere to be seen.

Suddenly, rising into view, then plunging out of sight again, they glimpsed—or did they imagine it?—a ship! "They'll never see us!" sobbed Hiroshi. But a wave picked them up and almost threw them against the side of the ship. And there, reaching down, were weathered brown hands, grabbing at the slippery wetness of their hair!

It was one of those ocean rivers that had swept Hiroshi out to sea. The ship's skipper told them so when he had brought them both safe home.

"They're longer than any river on dry land," he said. "They carried our ancestors' tiny boats all around the world, some to live here, some to settle there . . ."

"You mean that Pablo's ancestors and ours might have lived in the same place once?" exclaimed Akiko. "Might have been brothers, even?"

"Well, of course! We're all just sailors come ashore off the same deep blue sea!"

"Maybe that's why I rowed out when I saw Hiroshi was in trouble," said Pablo. "How can brothers be enemies?"

"How can *anyone* be enemies," said Hiroshi, "if it's only the sea in between that makes us different?"

"Sometimes people forget," said the skipper sadly. Like Pablo's grandma, he could remember the war

"Sometimes people forget . . ."

Not Akiko, nor Pablo, nor Hiroshi. They would not forget what the sea and the skipper had taught them. So, on the day he sailed away, three children waved good-bye from the shore; three good friends, not enemies; three sailors come ashore off the same deep blue sea.

That same night the turtles' eggs hatched, and the baby turtles, guided by the sea's shine, tumbled into the water at the start of their own lifetime of voyaging along the oceans' rivers.

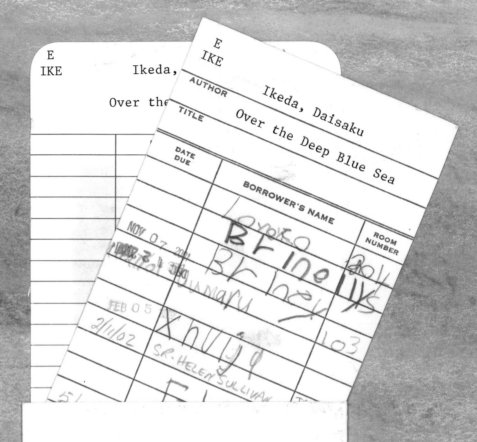